LIGHTHOUSE ISLAND

LIGHTHOUSE ISLAND

By Elizabeth Coatsworth

Illustrated by Symeon Shimin

W·W·NORTON & COMPANY·INC·NEW YORK

BY ELIZABETH COATSWORTH

Lighthouse Island

Cricket and the Emperor's Son

Troll Weather

The Place

The Cat Who Went to Heaven

Ronnie and the Chief's Son

Alice All-By-Herself

The Captain's Daughter

The Cat and the Captain

The Little Haymakers

Sword of the Wilderness

Away Goes Sally

The Fair American

Five Bushel Farm

The Wishing Pear

Boston Bells

Old Whirlwind

The Sod House

The Sparrow Bush

Poems

Summer Green

for Harriet Buchheister,

who knows and loves

the Rock so well

U NTIL 1939, at the time of the Second World War, lighthouses were under control of the United States Lighthouse Service and most of them were run by keepers with families, as they had been from the time they were built. Now they are administered by the Coast Guard Service and although there are still a few family lighthouses left here and there, many of them are either in charge of Coast Guardsmen—often young men from the inland states—or are directed by remote control, while the houses beside the white towers stand empty.

But when Alex came to Lighthouse Island off the coast of Maine, his Uncle Bill was light-house keeper with two assistants, and his Aunt Madge was the only woman on the island and loved her small kingdom. The trip from Ohio, first by train, then by mail boat, and finally by

lobster boat, had been long and tiring though
exciting, too. But at last when Alex saw the
Rock (as the island was usually called) rising
out of the sea, like the back of a gray whale, he
couldn't believe that this treeless, windblown,
speck of stone could be where he was expected

to spend the whole summer. Even getting on shore wasn't easy, for there was no natural landing place, and Fred Young, the lobsterman who had brought him on the last lap of his trip, had to maneuver his boat onto a wooden slip leading to the boathouse, with the help of the two assistant keepers.

"Lots of days you can't land here at all," said Fred. "You're lucky."

If Alex was lucky, he didn't feel so. He got out slowly, looking around in a daze. He scarcely saw the two young keepers but he shook hands with them and thanked them and said good-bye to Fred and followed the assistants up steep steps to the top of the island, if you could call it an island.

There Alex met his Uncle Bill for the first time. He was a big man with blue eyes. They shook hands, and then Alex was hugged by his Aunt Madge, a small woman who ran out of the house, drying her hands on her apron. As far as Alex could tell, they seemed very nice. One of the assistants helped him carry his suitcase and duffel bag upstairs to his room. But Alex felt too miserable to stay there, so down he came, past the kitchen door where he could hear Aunt Madge moving about, and out through the front door.

Fred's boat, returning to the larger island from which it had come, was already almost lost in the endless glare of the water. It was too far away for waving. Uncle Bill and the assistants had disappeared. There was no one in sight.

"So here I am," Alex thought, kicking a loose pebble, "on the Rock. And I'm here for the whole summer."

All about him lay the ocean—nothing but water and waves. All above him stretched the sky—with a roof of angry seabirds flying overhead, screaming and darting down at him, snapping their red-lined bills. He stood in a tumble of rocks with a few wild angelica plants between them. There wasn't a tree of any sort, not even a bush. To one side rose the tall lighthouse. To the other side stood the gray houses of the keepers, in the larger of which Aunt Madge at that moment was cooking dinner.

There wasn't another boy on the Rock.

11

There wasn't a dog. There wasn't so much as a
cat. There were only these scolding birds called
terns in a white cloud above him, and under-
foot were their eggs and chicks, some lying in
hollows in the rock and some among the
clumps of coarse grass and weeds growing

12

here and there. Alex had to be careful where
he stepped. But the terns didn't think he knew
enough to be careful.

"Go away! Go away! Go away!" they
screamed in tern talk, and circled and dived at
his head, snapping their sharp beaks.

13

What was he supposed to do? Back home his big brother John would be doing something interesting, or Alex could get Ann or Barbara, his sisters, to play ball with him, or he could hunt up one of his friends down the street. And at home he had a bicycle. And his father had a car. But here on the Rock there wasn't even a corner store, let alone a chance to go to the movies. There'd be no buses, no traffic, no people passing by along the sidewalks. There'd be no fire sirens and no church bells on Sunday mornings. He'd never hear a train hoot, nor a car honk at a crossing.

Sun and sky and sea and wind and the Rock! Clouds and waves and terns, the lighthouse and the keepers' houses—how gladly he'd trade them all for an hour back home again! Very gloomily, Alex decided to unpack his things.

As he came in, shutting the front door rather hard behind him, Aunt Madge called to him cheerfully from the kitchen and Alex politely called back as he went up the steep stairs. His little room faced the lighthouse tower. Its walls were painted stone gray and the floor was a darker gray. There was a bright braided rug beside the bed with its white coverlet, a plain bureau and washstand and two straight-backed chairs. That was all, except for an old-fashioned print called "The Cabin Boy's Return." The cabin boy must have been about Alex's age, but he was dressed like a real sailor, in blue bell-bottom trousers, a white shirt, and flowing tie. However, the most interesting thing about him was the big parrot on his shoulder, showing that he'd been to all sorts of exciting places. Alex stood quite a while looking at the picture and pretending that he was the cabin boy. Then reluctantly, he unpacked his shirts and shorts and sweaters and shoes, looked at the cabin boy again, and went down to sit in the kitchen to watch Aunt Madge get supper. Later he ate supper with his uncle and aunt and the two young keepers, who were friendly, but rather silent, because they were doing more eating than talking.

That night, when his light was turned out, Alex discovered something else about his room, and that was the lighthouse light. There was no getting away from it. First there would be a few seconds of darkness. Then a blinding light would sweep slowly across his room, and then across his face. Then it would feel along the gray wall opposite and then it was gone. But it would be right back again. It moved in a regular rhythm: one four three. Aunt Madge, poking her head in at the door to say goodnight, told him that people said it spelled

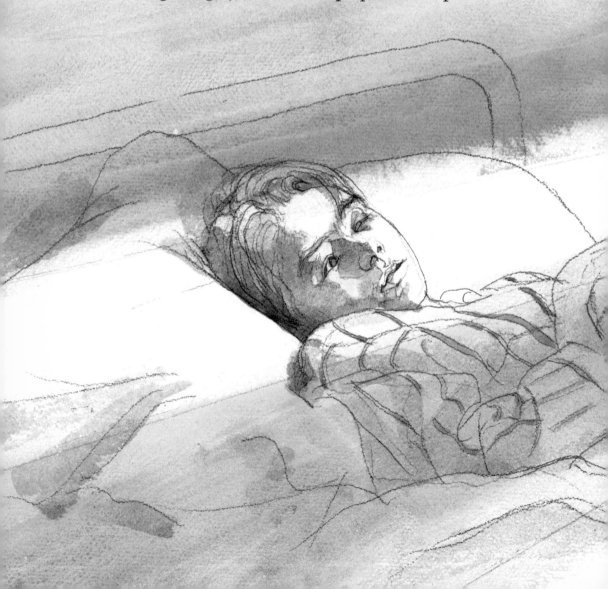

out: "I L-O-V-E Y-O-U." But later that night Alex, his head half under the covers, muttered, "I H-A-T-E Y-O-U!" to the light.

"I'll be awake all night," he grumbled. "Why did I ever come to this dumb place?"

But Alex was too tired to stay awake very long. Grumbling and muttering, he was soon asleep, and after the first few nights he never noticed the light again nor even the foghorn which blew whenever the fog came in, blotting out the world, soaking Aunt Madge's laundry on the line, and stilling even the wind, which seemed to have its headquarters on the island.

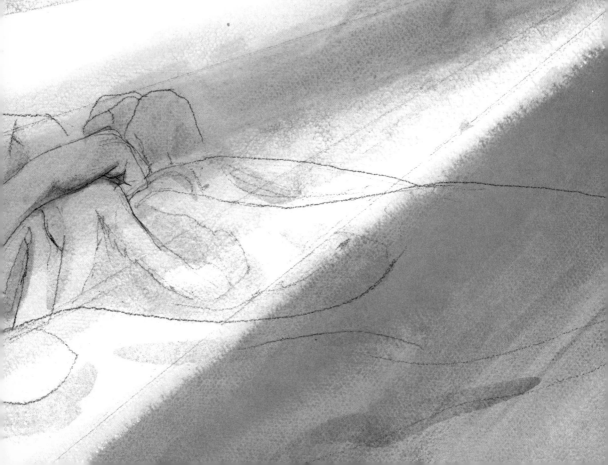

The next morning, the Rock didn't seem quite so bad. There was the smell of salt-and-seaweed in the air and the splash and gurgle of water among the boulders that Alex would have liked, if he'd had a friend to share it with. He went exploring among the jumble of slabs. On the side facing Spain, the island fell away to the sea in a fifty-foot cliff. On the mainland side, it sloped more gradually toward the water and it was here that Alex found the wreck of a lobster boat with *Annie S.* painted on her bow. The hull was stove in and the engine gone, but he could sit at the stern, and at the bow there was a half-cabin where some lobsterman had once stood by the steering wheel. Storms had washed seaweed and bits of floating wood and crab shells into the cockpit, but that first day Alex did nothing about them.

At this end of the island there were no terns shrieking and dive-bombing at him, but he

noticed another kind of bird. They were black and white, in dress suits like penguins, but with enormous blue and red and yellow bills. Stranger still, they had big pale rings around their eyes which made them look like parrots in goggles. One by one, they'd fly in from the sea and light on the peaks of the rock slabs. They always had two or three or even four little fishes in their bills and usually the little fishes' heads faced the same way. After sitting for a while, looking around, a bird would patter down the side of the slab and dive out of sight between the rocks. When it came out, it wouldn't have any fish. It would climb back solemnly to the top of its roof and then, pouf! off it would fly again to fish among the endless waves. These birds weren't like the terns. They didn't seem afraid, and they didn't seem suspicious. Perhaps they knew Alex couldn't step on their babies because each solitary chick was safe far down in its own igloo of rock.

That evening at supper Alex had a lot of questions to ask Uncle Bill.

"Did the men on the *Annie S.* get drowned?" was the first question. "And how did she get wrecked?" he went on before Uncle Bill could answer. Uncle Bill was a slow man and always took his time. He finished buttering a piece of hot corn bread, and took a bite or two.

Then he said, "Had engine trouble and started to pile up on the island. It was a half gale of wind and the sea was picketty. Happened that none of us at the station had seen that the *Annie S.* was in difficulties. First thing we knew, Jason Ames and his brother, Eldridge, came bursting into the kitchen here, looking like death. Seems their craft came on

the rocks, bow first. Happened the bow got wedged in the boulders and gave them time to jump ashore between breakers. Mighty ticklish business, big as those breakers were.''

"They were lucky," said Aunt Madge. "I can't remember how many mugs of hot coffee they drank. Seemed like I couldn't fill them up."

"They were lucky," Uncle Bill repeated in his slow way. "The *Annie S.* had the name of being a lucky boat. Seems as if when she couldn't make it out to sea, she did what she could for Jason and Eldridge. They've named their new boat *Annie S. II.* Of course the *Annie* was all stove up during the night, but they salvaged the engine."

The young assistants had finished eating. They excused themselves and went out.

Uncle Bill went back to his corn bread and for a few minutes Alex was content to eat while he thought over what he'd heard.

Then he said, "There were some strange birds with big bills like parrots."

"Yes," said Aunt Madge, "I like them, too. There's always a colony of puffins on that side

24

of the island."

"Most people just call them sea parrots," Uncle Bill said.

"Can they talk?" asked Alex.

"Not that I ever heard tell," said Uncle Bill. "But they're friendly. They'd talk if they could."

"Why are they friendly?"

"Why are chicadees friendly? Chicadees will follow you through the woods as if they liked company. And robins almost always build near houses. I don't know why. Do you, Madge?"

"I think chipping sparrows are maybe the friendliest of all, but I don't know why," said Aunt Madge.

Alex had never wondered much about birds before. He wondered a good deal, later on, but just now he was busy saying to himself, "puff-in, puff-out, puff-out, puff-in," as he ate. The name, puffin, sounded funny, just like the birds.

ONE morning, a few weeks later, the station launch went to the mainland with an assistant keeper and, when it came back, it brought a big nanny goat followed by a kid as white as a cloud. Alex liked her the moment he laid eyes on her. She jumped from rock to rock, and her feet made a little click like dancing. She had two natural silky white bells at her throat, and her eyes were pale and clear. She wouldn't stand still, but frolicked about her mother as the keeper led the big goat up to the house where Aunt Madge was waiting with a pan of oats.

"A very nice nanny you are," said Aunt Madge to the mother goat. "Are you surprised, Alex? I've been hankering for fresh milk for a long time. Any cow would break her leg here in five minutes, but it's just the place for a goat, and the kid is old enough now to get along without much milk. Don't try to make friends too fast, Alex. Give them time to look around and get their bearings. In a little while you can give the kid some dry bread and get acquainted."

It wasn't long before the white kid was following Alex wherever he went, and that's why he called her Tagalong. When he explored among the tumbled rocks, Tagalong went exploring, too, poking her narrow nose into everything. She, too, was careful not to step on the terns' nests or on their pretty chicks, but little good it did her in the terns' eyes. They dived and screamed at Tagalong just as they dived and screamed at Alex, and both were glad to hurry away to the peaceful side of the Rock where the puffins lived.

Here they spent hours in and about the *Annie S.* pretending to go on cruises to all the

28

harbors of the world. Alex liked to curl up in the stern, but Tagalong chose to stand at the bow on the roof of the `cabin, because she always liked high places best. If Alex stayed quiet too long, she'd go exploring, usually to the puffins' special ridge where they sat when they weren't fishing or feeding their chicks. At first, when she came near, the puffins flew away on their short busy wings, but after a few days they didn't seem to mind Tagalong at all. And after a few weeks they even seemed to like her. Alex thought that when Tagalong was standing on the puffins' ridge, more birds than usual gathered, perching in twos or threes like courtiers around their queen. Then, when at last Tagalong wandered down to the water's edge, the puffins would fly away to their fishing.

Alex made up a rhyme which he sang to his own tune:

> I saw a puffin,
> Stuffin' and stuffin'
> On an old buttered muffin.

"What you doin', puffin,
Gobblin' and stuffin'
On that silly old muffin?"

It seemed to Alex that while he sang, all the puffins sat up straighter than ever, proudly looking down their big many-colored beaks.

"Who says that I'm stuffin'?"
Asks that puffed-up puffin,
"I'm not doing nuffin'!"

"Besides," says the puffin,
"It's an awful good muffin!"

Alex thought his song was very funny. The puffins, of course, didn't understand, but they seemed to enjoy having Alex sing to them. They were a good deal of company, friendly company, not like the bad-tempered terns. As for Tagalong, they even allowed her to poke them with her nose, and they didn't seem to mind when Alex stuck his head into their igloos to see their solitary, ugly chicks.

When Tagalong went down to the water's edge, she had a reason, for there at low tide she could nibble the seaweed growing along the edge of the water which she loved better than any other food.

There was one favorite stretch of flat rock that appeared only at very low tide. Near the shore it began with a tide pool and then came a stretch of green slippery rock and then a boulder, three or four feet high, squatting like a wet green frog at the edge of the sea. Tagalong loved to feed along this flat rock which made a small green sea-pasture with starfish and urchins instead of flowers. Once Alex tried to go with her, but he slipped on the seaweed and landed on his back with a splash, and after that he watched her from the shore. When at last he wandered away, Tagalong would follow rather unwillingly, taking a few last hasty bites as she went.

Once in a while, if the water wasn't too rough, Alex had a chance to go out fishing in the station launch with one of the assistants. When he asked about catching lobsters he was told that the water near the Rock was too deep, but the next time the launch went to the mainland for supplies, it came back with a sackful of live lobsters—great green creatures plated in armor like knights, with wooden pegs in their claws to keep them from fighting with one another. They were goblin things, like the crayfish Alex had found under rocks in Ohio streams, but very, very, very much larger.

Uncle Bill dipped up some ocean water to steam them in. Alex couldn't imagine eating one, but when Aunt Madge served them that evening, piping hot and bright red, with melted butter, he found that he liked them very much —at least, after the first few bites.

By this time Alex had cleared out the sand and debris from the hull of the *Annie S.*, for he wanted her shipshape when he went cruising to far-off lands. He was also collecting earth for a little garden, digging some of it up from between rocks and asking the assistant keepers to bring back a bucketful when they went on shore leave. Around his plot he built a fence and put in lettuce seeds and six pansy plants, which the younger assistant brought him as a present, and soon he had fresh lettuce for salads and enough flowers for a very small bouquet for Aunt Madge.

Nowadays, too, he spent more time in the lighthouse tower, talking to Uncle Bill as he helped him clean the endless brasswork in the lantern, or went out with him on the catwalk to polish the glass windows. At first he felt a

little dizzy up so high with only a narrow rail between him and the drop to the rocks and the sea below, but he soon got used to it.

"You should be here when we whitewash the tower," Uncle Bill said. "We're like steeple-jacks hanging in a swing slung from the lantern railing. We choose a still day, you can be sure of that! The real daisy of a job is putting the black paint on the lantern dome. I'm too old for going up there. One of the younger men volunteers and we all stand around holding our breath until he gets it done."

"Sometimes you stay up here in the lantern all night, don't you, Uncle Bill?" Alex asked.

Uncle Bill shook his head. "Usually we keepers take turns keeping an eye on things. I stay up all night only in very foggy or very stormy weather to make sure myself that the incandescent oil vapor is feeding into the lamp properly, and that the reflectors are turning, and the foghorn machinery running smoothly. If anything went out of order for even five minutes, lives might be lost out there." And Uncle Bill glanced over his shoulder at the sea.

"Why is the Rock out here all by itself away from the other islands, Uncle Bill?"

"It's the top of a drowned mountain. This whole coast is sinking. Some day there may *be* no Rock. Only a shoal with waves breaking over it."

Alex looked uneasy.

"Oh, not in our time," said Uncle Bill. "Not for thousands of years. Maybe more. No one knows how long ago the Rock stopped being a mountain top and became an island. And whatever was on top of the mountain when it happened, had to stay here. I've heard that on some islands an animal or a plant or an insect will develop down the years so that it's different from any other of its kind in the world. No one's ever studied the plants and insects on the Rock. There might be ants with feelers just a little bit different from an ant's feelers any other place."

"Could our puffins or terns be different?" Alex asked hopefully.

Uncle Bill shook his head. "No, they're just summer visitors, like you," he said. "The puf-

fins, now, when their chicks can fly, scatter
along the coast. They don't go very far. But
the terns! They say that the terns migrate farther than any other bird. They fly north first
and then cross the Atlantic to Europe and then
fly southward down the coast to Africa, and
then down, down to the Antarctic, and there
they winter—of course, it's the Antarctic sum-

mer—among the glaciers and ice floes, and next spring they'll be back on the Rock."

"Wow!" said Alex. So that's what the terns did. Farther than any other bird in the world! When school opened, he'd go back to Ohio, but the terns, why, the terns would go to the Antarctic and see whales and penguins and all sorts of wonderful things.

Speaking of wonderful things, at that very moment a whale blew to the lee of the Rock and then another and another and another. There must have been at least four of them, so near the island that Alex could hear the rush of the vapor rising in fountains above them.

There he stood, on the platform outside the lighthouse lantern, the sea breeze blowing past him, the sky misty, the sea almost still, and the great whales passing by the Rock, which had once been a mountain top.

That afternoon Alex fell fast asleep curled up in the stern of the *Annie S.* And he dreamed that he was sailing under an umbrella of terns which flew over him screaming, steering their flight with their tails, forked like a swallow's, and sometimes they dived straight down like falling plummets, disappearing under the waves for a second, to rise out again with a fish in their bills.

On and on they went and Tagalong was standing at the very bow of the *Annie S.* like a white figurehead, and there were sails, too, instead of an engine, and Alex knew just what to do with the sails, for he wasn't himself at all, but the cabin boy in his picture, only instead of a parrot on his shoulder, there was a puffin.

North they went and then east, across the Atlantic, down the coast of Portugal and Spain, and down and down, past Gibraltar, until they saw Africa and the Atlas mountains and green jungles and white beaches, and now they weren't alone, for a great gray whale swam on either side of the *Annie S.*, blowing fountains of spray into the sunny air and steadying the boat in rough weather, pressing their great

sides against the hull, so that it wouldn't roll.

But it was getting cold. And now there was a gleam of icy mountains, and pack ice drifted past them and the terns screamed for joy and seemed never to tire of their diving.

And at last Alex could understand their talk and their cries of delight.

"But why do you want to spend the winter in this cold place among all this ice and snow?" he asked.

And they screamed back at him. "Because! because! because! silly! It's summer here! We don't care about ice and snow as long as we have all these FISHES!"

Their voices were just as sharp and scolding as ever, and with that last loud cry of "FISHES!" Alex woke up, and there he was in his usual clothes, curled up in the *Annie S.* with Tagalong in her favorite place at the bow, and a puffin perched on a nearby rock, and a few visiting terns screaming overhead. A fog was coming in, chilling the sunlight. As he and Tagalong clambered back to the station, the sun turned to a silver dollar and then was gone, leaving the Rock alone in the heaving sea, so that when the foghorn began, it seemed to be the voice of the island itself, lost and despairing.

In August there was a great deal of fog and the air was damp and chilly and Alex was glad to wear his sweater. The terns seemed even more restless than usual. Their fledglings were now able to fly and Uncle Bill said that pretty soon they'd be leaving. The puffins hadn't far to go, so they weren't thinking about leaving yet, though early in September flocks of little shore birds stopped at the Rock for a few days on their way south. But the most unexpected visitors were the orange milkweed butterflies.

"How can a butterfly get out here?" Alex wondered. "They never seem to know where they're going, but here they come, one by one, flying so low over all this water."

Uncle Bill said they were called monarchs and were migrating, just like the birds, and that they, too, in their fluttering, uncertain way, traveled hundreds of miles to the south.

"How do they know where to go?" Alex asked.

"How does anything know?" Uncle Bill said thoughtfully. "How does one flower know it's to be pink and another one that it's to be yellow and another one that it's to be blue, though they all grow from the same earth? How does one feather know it's to have a white spot on it? How does an eel find its way back from the middle of the ocean to its family pond?"

Aunt Madge had been listening and now she laughed.

"And how does your hair, Alex, grow an inch every time my back is turned? Sit down and let me clip it a little or your mother will think that we're sending back a wild boy."

47

IT was almost time for Alex to be leaving,
but he didn't want to leave. Life on the Rock
had become very important to him. He wanted
to go on discovering things, wondering about
things and asking questions, whether they
could be answered or not. He didn't want to
leave the Rock and the sun and the wind and
the fog and the endless changing voices of the
sea. And he didn't want to leave Uncle Bill and
Aunt Madge and Tagalong.

49

The day before Alex was to go, the wind was northwest and the weather was bright and clear. He saw a line of leaping porpoises playing in the meadows of the ocean. The sun

poured its living light down upon the Rock, that lost mountain top. The circling water splashed and gurgled about its foot as the tide began to turn, and he, Alex, went very unwillingly upstairs to pack.

"I'm coming back next year," he said to himself. "Uncle Bill and Aunt Madge have asked me, and the family says I may." He went to the window expecting to see Tagalong who usually waited outside for him. But today Tagalong wasn't there.

"Oh, well," thought Alex. "She's somewhere." And he went on packing, trying to do everything in lighthouse fashion, shipshape, to surprise his mother.

He was only half through when his attention was roused by the deep cries of puffins outside his window. "What are puffins doing on this side of the island?" Alex thought. "They never come over here into tern country." And next he thought, "Those are their alarm calls."

For a minute more he went on packing, but the cries continued. The puffins were wheeling over the house, calling and calling.

"You'd think they were trying to tell me something," Alex thought uneasily. "Could there be anything wrong?"

It was hard to think what could be wrong. Perhaps puffins always circled and cried like this when they were getting ready to leave the

island. But why should they wheel just over the house? And why should they sound so desperate?

Alex left his packing and galloped down the stairs and out the door.

As soon as they caught sight of him, the puffins redoubled their cries, and that, too, seemed strange.

Alex, shading his eyes with one hand, watched them. They were still wheeling, but now the circle was drifting away from the building toward puffin-land and the *Annie S.* Alex followed slowly, sometimes watching them and sometimes keeping an eye on his footing. He passed his little garden where one pansy plant was still in bloom. He passed the ridge where the puffin club liked to meet, but today there wasn't a bird on it. He passed the *Annie S.* and still the puffins led him on. Now suddenly he heard another sound. It was the terrified bleating of Tagalong.

After that, Alex needed no puffins to guide him. He scrambled and stumbled to the end of the island and there stood Tagalong, perched on the farthest froglike boulder in the midst of

55

the incoming tide. All about her shouldered the smooth green water. She must have been so busy browsing on salt seaweed that she hadn't noticed when the pool between her and the

Rock began to fill and overflow. She must have
gone on eating greedily until she was com-
pletely cut off from shore and then, as the
water crept up a little at a time, she had re-

treated to the final boulder that, for a little while, was still high and dry above the returning sea.

Her bleatings, loud as they were, were not loud enough to reach human ears at the station. Even her mother in the yard by the back door had not taken alarm. But the puffins had known that she was in danger. How did they know? How much did they know? What affection stirred in their bird hearts to send them off to get human help?

Now they perched on various outcroppings as if they were watching to see what Alex would do, their own part of the rescue ended.

A month ago Alex would have rushed into the water, forgetting how slippery the flats were, forgetting that the flow of the tide might drag him off his feet. But now he called encouragement to Tagalong and then stood thinking.

He remembered that there was an old line coiled on the deck of the *Annie S*. He must get that first. And he must find a boulder heavy enough to hold his weight, but small enough to tie the line around. And he must make a good knot. This was no time for a knot to slip. Even three weeks ago he would not have known how to do it, but one rainy afternoon the assistant keepers had given him a lesson in knots, and now he remembered what he had learned.

The other end he must fasten about his waist, leaving his hands free. And he must keep calm and walk slowly and carefully.

The puffins all stared at Alex solemnly as he waded out into the water and Tagalong bleated more piercingly than ever.

Once Alex slipped but regained his footing. Once he fell and went forward on his hands and knees until the water grew deeper and he could hoist himself upright with the help of his rope. Fortunately for him there was no wind. The force of the sea was there, but it was a quiet force.

As Alex came near the boulder, Tagalong suddenly launched herself with a great splash into the water to meet him. Given courage by his presence, bleating and striking out with her little hoofs, she swam along at his side. For

59

Alex, the return was easier than the outward trip, for he could now use the rope to steady himself. In no time the two were pulling themselves out on dry land, panting, dripping, and safe.

The puffins eyed them thoughtfully, in their usual silence. If Tagalong thanked them for their help, it was in a way that Alex could not understand. Alex thanked them in words, but they gave no sign of understanding him.

The puffins' work was done. Now they had only to doze in the sun until they felt like eating another little fish.

When Alex and Tagalong reached the station, Aunt Madge sent Alex upstairs to change his clothes, while she dried Tagalong with an old bath towel at the back step.

"There!" she said when she was through, getting up and opening the gate of the goat yard. "In you go! And from now on you stay with your mama and behave yourself. Next summer it will be a different story. You'll be able to go wherever you please when Alex and the puffins are back again on the Rock to keep an eye on you!"

Hearing Aunt Madge's words through his half-open window, Alex smiled at the picture of the cabin boy.

"Next summer," he told him, "I'll be coming back, too. Just like you." And for a moment he saw himself in bell-bottom trousers and a ribboned sailor's hat, with a parrot on his shoulder. The vision faded, but the important thing remained: he was coming back.

About the Author

Elizabeth Coatsworth is the author of more than fifty books for young people. Some of her most recent books are *Bess and the Sphinx, Cricket and the Emperor's Sons,* and *The Sparrow Bush,* a collection of poetry. Miss Coatsworth received the Newbery Medal for her book *The Cat Who Went to Heaven,* and she was recently runner-up for the Hans Christian Andersen Medal, awarded for a lifetime contribution to children's literature. *Lighthouse Island* reflects her love of New England, where she and her husband, Henry Beston, brought up their children. Miss Coatsworth's home is in Nobleboro, Maine.

About the Illustrator

Symeon Shimin is one of the finest illustrators working in the children's book field today. He is also a well-known painter. Mr. Shimin was born in Russia and came to America in 1912. He is the illustrator of *Listen Rabbit, One Small Blue Bead, Sam, The Man Who Talked to a Tree,* and *Zeely.* He lives with his family in New York City.

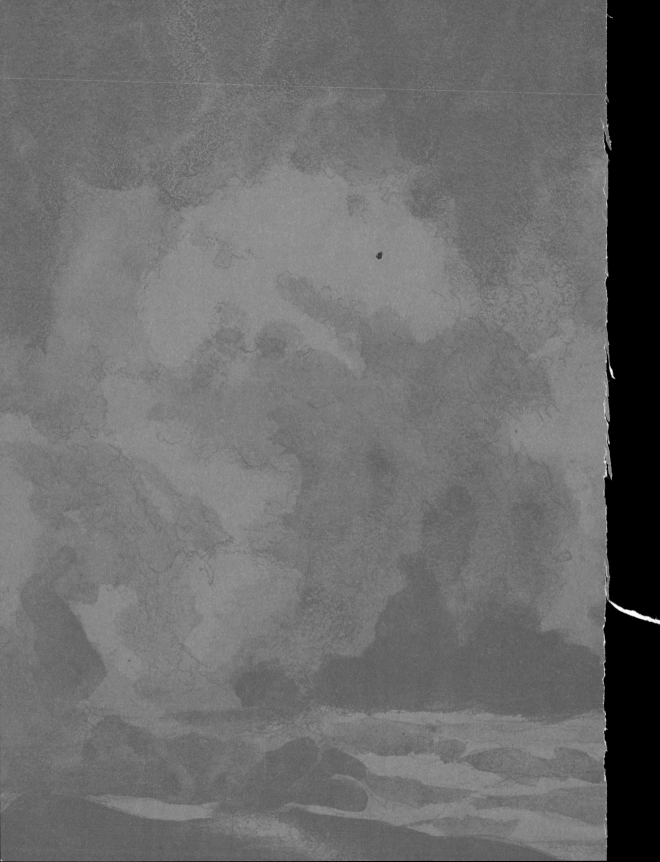